Spotty Leopard's Birthday Party Picnic Surprise

Spotty Leopard's Birthday Party Picnic Surprise

by

Michael Kamplain

Illustrations by Jonathan Harper

Xulon Press Elite

Xulon Press Elite
2301 Lucien Way #415
Maitland, FL 32751
407.339.4217
www.xulonpress.com

Unless otherwise indicated, Scripture quotations taken from the English Standard Version (ESV). Copyright © 2001 by Crossway, a publishing ministry of Good News Publishers. Used by permission. All rights reserved.

Printed in the United States of America.

Paperback ISBN-13: 978-1-6628-0972-9
Ebook ISBN-13: 978-1-6628-0973-6

Special Thanks

I would like to thank my wonderful wife Melodye for
encouraging me to write this book. Her love for Perrie
is expressed in the editing and suggestions that
helped bring the characters to life.

Introduction

There is a special place in every grandparent's heart for their grandchildren. Our granddaughter, Perrie Grace, struck a chord with my wife Melodye and I when she was born and has continued to play on our heartstrings ever since. This book celebrates the times that I have spent enjoying conversations with Perrie in her tree swing learning about her honest love for God and her simple childlike faith. I hope that readers will love and appreciate this sweet tale of Perrie as Spotty Leopard and all of her special friends.

Proverbs 17:6 "Children's children are a crown to the aged, and parents are the pride of their children."

The Back Story

There once was a little girl named Perrie Grace. One day during one of her many conversations with her grandfather, Papi, she talked to him about putting a swing in a tree for her. Papi liked the idea, but when he looked up in the trees, he could not find a good limb on which to hang a swing. Papi thought about it. He prayed about it. Finally an idea came to him. He knew just how to make it work. "Praise the Lord!" he shouted. He took a long wooden pole and laid it on two strong limbs that were in two pine trees. He then hung the swing on the pole with two strong ropes. He tested it to make sure it would be safe. Up and down, back and forth went the swing. Oh! It was just right.

When Perrie arrived the next day, the first thing she saw was the shiny red and blue swing. "Papi, you did it!", She exclaimed! She was so happy. She jumped up and down and clapped her hands. Papi lifted her into the swing and she smiled. She felt so safe and snug. Perrie looked up into the tall pine trees and saw how big they were. As Papi gently pushed the swing, she closed her eyes and her imagination began to soar. She wondered, "Is this what it is like to be a bird in the sky or is this how butterflies feel when they fly from flower to flower?" "Papi!" "Please sing and tell me a story," she said sweetly. Papi loved to make up silly songs and stories. Perrie loves animals and sometimes she likes to dress up like her favorite imaginary friend, Spotty Leopard. Papi began singing about Spotty Leopard and her friends and this is where the story begins.

Spotty Leopard's
Birthday Party Picnic Surprise

One morning when Spotty Leopard woke up, she remembered it was her birthday. She thought to herself, "Will there be a party?" "Will there be cake?" "Who will come to my party?" She quickly ran downstairs and saw mom and dad fixing breakfast, "Good morning Spotty," they said. Her little brother was playing with his toys and said hi Spotty. But no one said, happy birthday.

She started to feel sad and wondered if anyone even remembered it was her birthday. She sat down to breakfast with her family and her dad said a prayer of thanks and they began to eat. Spotty got sadder and sadder but did not say anything. After breakfast, Spotty helped with the dishes, she was hoping someone would say happy birthday. She quietly went to the living room and sat in her favorite chair when suddenly she heard a knock, knock, knock on the door.

When she opened it, there stood her friends, Bootsy Cat, Rainbow Butterfly and Mike Monkey.

All of her family and friends shouted, "Surprise!". "Happy Birthday Spotty", Bootsy said, "Are you ready to go Spotty?"

'What?" "Where are we going?", asked Spotty. "We have an amazing day planned for you." Bootsy said happily. Spotty was so excited she jumped up and down and clapped her paws. "You better bring your red wagon. We are going to Uncle Matt Mongoose's store to get food for your special birthday picnic at Pine Tree Park." Bootsy said.

On their way, they hopped and jumped and skipped. When they got there, they picked out their favorite foods to take to the picnic party. Spotty picked her favorite food, cottage cheese with peaches and Bootsy picked cat snacks. Rainbow Butterfly picked pollen and Mike Monkey picked pears. After they paid Uncle Matt, they went outside and placed their goodies in Spotty's little red wagon.

Bootsy was very excited because she knew the party was going to be so much fun. As they were walking along toward the park, they were approached by another friend, Angie Aardvark. "Hey where are you all going?" she asked.

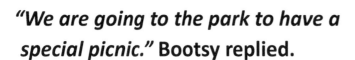

"We are going to the park to have a special picnic." Bootsy replied.

Angie asked, "May I come along too?"

Together Spotty and Bootsy answered, "of course!" "Well," said Mike Monkey with a playful look. "If you want to come along, will you join us in song? Will you say please, and will you please cover your sneeze? Can you bring a snack to share and we always offer a thankful prayer."

'I will!" Angie replied. "How about I bring a-a-avocadoes?" she asked with a smile." Everyone was thrilled and said yes.

Another friend, Baxter Baboon, came by and said, "Hey, where are you all going?"

"We are going to the park to have a special picnic." Bootsy replied.

Baxter asked, "May I come along?"

Together Spotty and Bootsy answered, "of course!" "Well," said Mike Monkey with a playful look. "If you want to come along, will you join us in song? Will you say please, and will you please cover your sneeze? Can you bring a snack to share and we always offer a thankful prayer."

"I will!" Baxter replied. "How about I bring b-b-bananas?" he asked with a smile." Everyone was thrilled and said yes.

Another friend, Carla Camel, came by and said "Hey, where are you all going?"

'We are going to the park to have a special picnic." Bootsy replied.

Carla asked, "May I come along?"

Together Spotty and Bootsy answered, "of course!" "Well," said Mike Monkey with a playful look. "If you want to come along, will you join us in song? Will you say please, and will you please cover your sneeze? Can you bring a snack to share and we always offer a thankful prayer."

"I will," Carla replied. "How about I bring c-c-cantaloupe?" she asked with a smile." Everyone was thrilled and said yes.

Another friend, Derek Dog, came by and said, "Hey, where are you all going?"

"We are going to the park to have a special picnic." Bootsy replied.

Derek asked, "May I come along?"

Together Spotty and Bootsy answered, "of course!" "Well," said Mike Monkey with a playful look. "If you want to come along, will you join us in song? Will you say please, and will you please cover your sneeze? Can you bring a snack to share and we always offer a thankful prayer."

"I will!" Derek replied. "How about I bring d-d-donuts?" he asked with a smile." Everyone was thrilled and said yes.

Another friend, Elias Eagle, flew by and said, "Hey, where are you all going?"

"We are going to the park to have a special picnic." Bootsy replied.

Elias asked, "May I come along?"

Together Spotty and Bootsy answered, "of course!" "Well," said Mike Monkey with a playful look. "If you want to come along, will you join us in song? Will you say please, and will you please cover your sneeze? Can you bring a snack to share and we always offer a thankful prayer."

"I will!" Elias replied. "How about I bring e-e-elbow macaroni?" he asked with a smile." Everyone was thrilled and said yes.

Another friend, Felicia Fox, came by and said, "Hey, where are you all going?"

"We are going to the park to have a special picnic." Bootsy replied.

Felicia asked, "May I come along?"

Together Spotty and Bootsy answered, "of course!" "Well," said Mike Monkey with a playful look. "If you want to come along, will you join us in song? Will you say please, and will you please cover your sneeze? Can you bring a snack to share and we always offer a thankful prayer."

"I will!" Felicia replied. "How about I bring f-f-fruit cake?" she asked with a smile." Everyone was thrilled and said yes.

Another friend, Gary Gorilla, came by and said, "Hey, where are you all going?"

"We are going to the park to have a special picnic," Bootsy replied

Gary asked, "May I come along?"

Together Spotty and Bootsy answered, "of course!" "Well," said Mike Monkey with a playful look. "If you want to come along, will you join us in song? Will you say please, and will you please cover your sneeze? Can you bring a snack to share and we always offer a thankful prayer."

"I will!" Gary replied. "How about I bring g-g-grapes?" he asked with a smile." Everyone was thrilled and said yes.

Another friend, Holly Hedgehog, came by and said, "Hey, where are you all going?"

"We are going to the park to have a special picnic." Bootsy replied Holly asked, "May I come along?"

Together Spotty and Bootsy answered, "of course!" "Well," said Mike Monkey with a playful look. "If you want to come along, will you join us in song? Will you say please, and will you please cover your sneeze? Can you bring a snack to share and we always offer a thankful prayer."

"I will!" Holly replied. "How about I bring h-h-honey?" she asked with a smile." Everyone was thrilled and said yes.

Another friend, Inez Iguana, came by and said, "Hey, where are you all going?"

Bootsy told her, *"We are going to the park to have a special picnic."*

Inez asked, "May I come along?"

Together Spotty and Bootsy answered, "of course!" "Well," said Mike Monkey with a playful look. "If you want to come along, will you join us in song? Will you say please, and will you please cover your sneeze? Can you bring a snack to share and we always offer a thankful prayer."

"I will!" Inez replied. "How about I bring I-I- Idaho potatoes?" she asked with a smile." Everyone was thrilled and said yes.

Another friend, Jessica Jaguar, came by and said, "Hey, where are you all going?"

"We are going to the park to have a special picnic." Bootsy replied.

Jessica asked, "May I come along?"

Together Spotty and Bootsy answered, "of course!" "Well," said Mike Monkey with a playful look. "If you want to come along, will you join us in song? Will you say please, and will you please cover your sneeze? Can you bring a snack to share and we always offer a thankful prayer."

"I will!" Jessica replied. "How about I bring j-j-jam?" she asked with a smile." Everyone was thrilled and said yes.

Another friend, Kerri Kiwi, came by and said, "Hey, where are you all going?"

"We are going to the park to have a special picnic." Bootsy replied.

Kerry asked, "May I come along?"

Together Spotty and Bootsy answered, "of course!" "Well," said Mike Monkey with a playful look. "If you want to come along, will you join us in song? Will you say please, and will you please cover your sneeze? Can you bring a snack to share and we always offer a thankful prayer."

"I will!" Kerry replied. "How about I bring k-k- kiwi fruit?" she asked with a smile." Everyone was thrilled and said yes.

Another friend, Lonnie Lion, came by and said "Hey, where are you all going?"

"We are going to the park to have a special picnic." Bootsy replied.

Lonnie asked, "May I come along?"

Together Spotty and Bootsy answered, "of course!" "Well," said Mike Monkey with a playful look. "If you want to come along, will you join us in song? Will you say please, and will you please cover your sneeze? Can you bring a snack to share and we always offer a thankful prayer."

"I will!" Lonnie replied. "How about I bring l-l-lasagna?" he asked with a smile." Everyone was thrilled and said yes.

Another friend, Mimi Meerkat, came by and said, "Hey, where are you all going?"

Bootsy told her, *"We are going to the park to have a special picnic."*

Mimi asked, "May I come along?"

Together Spotty and Bootsy answered, "of course!" "Well," said Mike Monkey with a playful look. "If you want to come along, will you join us in song? Will you say please, and will you please cover your sneeze? Can you bring a snack to share and we always offer a thankful prayer."

"I will!" Mimi replied. "How about I bring m-m-mangos?" she asked with a smile." Everyone was thrilled and said yes.

Another friend, Ned Newt, came by and said, "Hey, where are you all going?"

"We are going to the park to have a special picnic." Bootsy replied.

Ned asked, "May I come along?"

Together Spotty and Bootsy answered, "of course!" "Well," said Mike Monkey with a playful look. "If you want to come along, will you join us in song? Will you say please, and will you please cover your sneeze? Can you bring a snack to share and we always offer a thankful prayer."

"I will!" Ned replied. "How about I bring n-n-nectarines?" he asked with a smile." Everyone was thrilled and said yes.

Another friend, Olivia Ostrich, came by and said, "Hey, where are you all going?"

"We are going to the park to have a special picnic." Bootsy replied.

Olivia asked, "May I come along?"

Together Spotty and Bootsy answered, "of course!" "Well," said Mike Monkey with a playful look. "If you want to come along, will you join us in song? Will you say please, and will you please cover your sneeze? Can you bring a snack to share and we always offer a thankful prayer."

"I will!" Olivia replied. "How about I bring o-o-olives?" she asked with a smile." Everyone was thrilled and said yes.

Another friend, Polly Parrot, came by and said, "Hey, where are you all going?"

"We are going to the park to have a special picnic." Bootsy replied.

Polly asked, "May I come along?"

Together Spotty and Bootsy answered, "of course!" "Well," said Mike Monkey with a playful look. "If you want to come along, will you join us in song? Will you say please, and will you please cover your sneeze? Can you bring a snack to share and we always offer a thankful prayer."

"I will!" Polly replied. "How about I bring p-p-pickles?" she asked with a smile." Everyone was thrilled and said yes.

Another friend, Quinn Quail came by and said, "Hey, where are you all going?"

"We are going to the park to have a special picnic." Bootsy replied

Quinn asked, "May I come along?"

Together Spotty and Bootsy answered, "of course!" "Well," said Mike Monkey with a playful look. "If you want to come along, will you join us in song? Will you say please, and will you please cover your sneeze? Can you bring a snack to share and we always offer a thankful prayer."

"I will!" Quinn replied. "How about I bring q-q-quinoa?" he asked with a smile." Everyone was thrilled and said yes.

Another friend, Reggie Rabbit, came by and said, "Hey, where are you all going?"

"We are going to the park to have a special picnic." Bootsy replied.

Reggie asked, "May I come along?"

Together Spotty and Bootsy answered, "of course!" "Well," said Mike Monkey with a playful look. "If you want to come along, will you join us in song? Will you say please, and will you please cover your sneeze? Can you bring a snack to share and we always offer a thankful prayer."

"I will!" Reggie replied. "How about I bring r-r-raspberries?" he asked with a smile." Everyone was thrilled and said yes.

Another friend, Squire Squirrel came by and said, "Hey, where are you all going?"

"We are going to the park to have a special picnic." Bootsy replied

Squire asked, "May I come along?"

Together Spotty and Bootsy answered, "of course!" "Well," said Mike Monkey with a playful look. "If you want to come along, will you join us in song? Will you say please, and will you please cover your sneeze? Can you bring a snack to share and we always offer a thankful prayer."

"I will!" Squire replied. "How about I bring s-s-strawberries?" he asked with a smile." Everyone was thrilled and said yes.

Another friend, Thomas Tiger came by and said, "Hey, where are you all going?"

"We are going to the park to have a special picnic." Bootsy replied.

Thomas asked, "May I come along?"

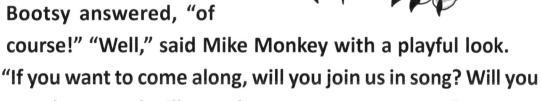

Together Spotty and Bootsy answered, "of course!" "Well," said Mike Monkey with a playful look. "If you want to come along, will you join us in song? Will you say please, and will you please cover your sneeze? Can you bring a snack to share and we always offer a thankful prayer."

"I will!" Thomas replied. "How about I bring t-t-tacos?" he asked with a smile." Everyone was thrilled and said yes.

Another friend, Una Unicorn came by and said, "Hey, where are you all going?"

"We are going to the park to have a special picnic." Bootsy replied.

Una asked, "May I come along?"

Together Spotty and Bootsy answered, "of course!" "Well," said Mike Monkey with a playful look. "If you want to come along, will you join us in song? Will you say please, and will you please cover your sneeze? Can you bring a snack to share and we always offer a thankful prayer."

"I will!" Una replied. "How about I bring u-u-upside down cake with sprinkles?" she asked with a smile." Everyone was thrilled and said yes.

Another friend, Victor Vulture came by and said, "Hey, where are you all going?"

"We are going to the park to have a special picnic." Bootsy replied

Victor asked, "May I come along?"

Together Spotty and Bootsy answered, "of course!" "Well," said Mike Monkey with a playful look. "If you want to come along, will you join us in song? Will you say please, and will you please cover your sneeze? Can you bring a snack to share and we always offer a thankful prayer."

"I will!" Victor replied. "How about I bring v-v-vanilla pudding?" he asked with a smile." Everyone was thrilled and said yes.

Another friend, Welles Whale, came swimming by and said, "Hey, where are you all going?"

"We are going to the park to have a special picnic." Bootsy replied

Welles asked, "May I come along?"

Together Spotty and Bootsy answered, "of course!" "Well," said Mike Monkey with a playful look. "If you want to come along, will you join us in song? Will you say please, and will you please cover your sneeze? Can you bring a snack to share and we always offer a thankful prayer."

"I will!" Welles replied. "How about I bring w-w-waffles?" he asked with a smile." Everyone was thrilled and said yes.

Another friend, X-Ray Fish, came swimming by and said, "Hey, where are you all going?"

"We are going to the park to have a special picnic." Bootsy replied.

X-Ray asked, "May I come along?"

Together Spotty and Bootsy answered, "of course!" "Well," said Mike Monkey with a playful look. "If you want to come along, will you join us in song? Will you say please, and will you please cover your sneeze? Can you bring a snack to share and we always offer a thankful prayer."

"I will!" X-Ray replied. "How about I bring x-x-Xylophone cookies?" she asked with a smile." Everyone was thrilled and said yes.

Another friend, Yolanda Yak came by and said, "Hey, where are you all going?"

"We are going to the park to have a special picnic." Bootsy replied

Yolanda asked, "May I come along?"

Together Spotty and Bootsy answered, "of course!" "Well," said Mike Monkey with a playful look. "If you want to come along, will you join us in song? Will you say please, and will you please cover your sneeze? Can you bring a snack to share and we always offer a thankful prayer."

"I will!" Yolanda replied. "How about I bring y-y-yams?" she asked with a smile." Everyone was thrilled and said yes.

The last friend, Zoe Zebra, came by and said, "Hey, where are you all going?"

"We are going to the park to have a special picnic." Bootsy replied.

Zoe asked, "May I come along?"

Together Spotty and Bootsy answered, "of course!" "Well," said Mike Monkey with a playful look. "If you want to come along, will you join us in song? Will you say please, and will you please cover your sneeze? Can you bring a snack to share and we always offer a thankful prayer."

"I will!" Zoe replied. "How about I bring z-z-zucchini?" she asked with a smile." Everyone was thrilled and said yes.

It didn't take long for Spotty's animal friends to get their food from Uncle Matt's Market for the party.

Spotty turned around and was surprised to see all of the animals that were following. It was like a big parade! Everyone was singing and laughing and having a great time together. Spotty turned to Bootsy and said, "I thought we were just having a little birthday picnic. This is huge!" As they got to the park, Spotty began hearing music. It was Larry the Lizard and the Blue Grass Frog Band. There were balloons, banners and a bounce house and games for all of Spotty's friends. There were also tables set up for all of the food and drinks. Spotty was full of joy.

She and all of her friends ran into the park and started having fun. They jumped and played and had a wonderful time.

Then Spotty's dad stood up and called everyone to gather at the tables.

He asked everyone to join him in prayer.

He prayed, "'This is the day that the Lord has made, we will rejoice and be glad in it.'" Thank you Lord for these friends and thank you for this food. Amen!"

After the party was over, Spotty said goodbye to all of her friends and thanked them once again for an amazing day. She went home with her family, took a bubble bath and put on her favorite pajamas. Her mom and dad tucked her and her little brother into bed and they said their prayers. All wrapped up in her favorite blanket and snuggled down in her warm bed, she could hardly stop thinking about what a fine large day it had been. It didn't take long until Spotty was fast asleep.

About the Author

Michael Kamplain is a working Pastor, college instructor and marriage and family counselor. He also works as a producer for a faith-based film company. He is a husband and father of two adult sons and has two grandchildren. The oldest grandchild is the inspiration for this book. He and his wife currently reside in Boise, Idaho close to their youngest son, his wife and their grandchildren.

About the Illustrator

Jonathan Harper is a freelance illustrator from a family of artists and musicians. He and his wife currently reside in Tuscaloosa, Alabama. He plans to further his education in the arts by attending an art school in the fall of 2022.

CPSIA information can be obtained
at www.ICGtesting.com
Printed in the USA
LVHW070623200721
693162LV00006B/117